To (the best) Grandma (ever) enjoy reading! Lots of Love,

Skylar :)

VIRIDIAN

BY STEPHY C

authorHOUSE®

AuthorHouse™ UK Ltd.
500 Avebury Boulevard
Central Milton Keynes, MK9 2BE
www.authorhouse.co.uk
Phone: 08001974150

© 2010 Stephy C. All rights reserved.

No part of this book may be reproduced, stored in a retrieval system, or transmitted by any means without the written permission of the author.

First published by AuthorHouse 2/26/2010

ISBN: 978-1-4490-5873-9 (sc)

This book is printed on acid-free paper.

ACKNOWLEDGMENT

I would like to thank, my friends and family. Especially my sister, Kk, who is the best sister anyone could ask for; my mom, who gave me unconditional love. My dad, who helped me financially; And J, who worked as my unpaid editor.

I'd also like to thank:
Adda, Hannah, Kate and Alison; for helping me read through my book and editing it. Also to Matthew.

The people who were involved with the production process at Author house;
Hannah Dibley
Caroline Haywood
Thames Team design team;
Ben Zemel

Thank you all so much. I hope you enjoy reading my book that you've all helped me to produce.

PREFACE

A tall brown haired man in an army uniform, loaned from a friend, marched through a wooded area. Charlie Fairbrother was a long way from home. Born in California he never thought he'd end up living in Arizona. Now he wasn't sure if he was still in Arizona, he just kept driving. Wilder back is a small town. If you drove fast enough you could go straight through and end up in the middle of no where.

His car was abandoned on the roadside somewhere. He found himself in a small forest. He had told his family that he'd been sent to Iraq. Lying to them was easy at first. He couldn't really get into the army of course because of his past. The secret that always lingered in the back of his mind. They were better off not knowing. They were safe that way. This was going to protect them.

Scanning the forest for clues, he found a stick snapped in half and footprints: Size nine and a half. He was here. Somewhere. He managed to stumble upon a small clearing. Long brownish grass bordered with trees. Plants seemed to avoid growing in the middle. It was dry and cracked. Tire tracks were carved into the dirt. Charlie's eyes followed them to a motionless blue Pontiac GTO

Charlie tried to keep his breathing and shaking hands under control. He swallowed hard. It didn't matter what happened to him; He had brought it on himself after all. "I should never have gotten involved with distributing drugs." He thought. "The money wasn't worth risking my future; But then again how was I suppose to know that twenty years later I'd have two beautiful daughters and a loving wife. I guess I figured I wouldn't settle down like everybody else."

Slam! A balding orange haired man stepped out of the car. He had gained weight and his clothes weren't as flashy. If it wasn't for his piercing green eyes Charlie wouldn't have recognized him. A suitcase was stuffed in the back of his car.

Mark stepped forward and Charlie noticed a drop of sweat trickle down his forehead. His eye's narrowed. Mark's hand disappeared into his coat pocket. It reappeared with a gun. Charlie knew this was coming. He knew coming here meant he was signing his death certificate. He was too proud to raise his hands

"You murderer!" Mark spat. "You killed my son...you killed Nick!"

"I never touched your son."

"You let the cat out..." "It's your fault he's dead and now I will have my revenge!" He hollered, his voice bouncing off the trees. The gun shook in his hand.

Anger bubbled in Charlie's stomach. "Then shoot me, Mark!" "Go ahead...do it!"

Suddenly, his feet fell out from under him. He was on his knees. Mark had kicked his legs. On the ground Mark's shadow swamped Charlie. Ringing blared in his ears. He squeezed his eyes together, trying to make it go away. It was something that had been happening to Charlie a lot lately. All of a sudden his ears would just ring. Mark's voice seemed to come out of nowhere. "He was my youngest!" He yelled. Click! He pulled back the hammer, ready to fire. "Now I come to find that you have kids of your own"

Charlie's eyelids sprung open. "..Now it will be your youngest!" Mark threatened.

"No! Not Brittany, she's only nine." "No..I'm the one you want, kill me!" He thought about begging, but he wasn't going to give Mark the pleasure. "I thought you came to kill me."

"I told you, I wanted revenge...and damn-it I will have it! Say good-bye to your little Brittany...don't worry, she will suffer!"

Bang...!

CHAPTER 1

EIGHT YEARS LATER

Misty rain spat in my face as I raced down the grey sidewalk. Bitter winds swept back my long blonde hair and kissed my cheeks with their freezing lips. Thump, thump, thump! The sound of footsteps pierced my ears. The shadows of the night followed my every move. The thought that someone was watching me grew stronger. The nights always come early in November. I began to wish I had taken the longer route home or asked Jace to walk the rest of the way with me.

My ribs began to ache. I slowed down, looking around as I did so. Gigantic oak trees looked down on me from both sides of the sidewalk. Suddenly my house felt so far away and the only comforting feeling in this dark place, was the evil smirks of the oak trees. The yellow street lamps flickered on and off. I turned to look behind me. No one was there, except the concrete river stretching through the forest, and the pitter patter of rain. Black clouds began to brew above and the rain slowly fell harder. A flicker of moonlight escaped. It outlined a black crow which sat on a branch. Silence.

Suddenly the bushes, in amongst the trees, rustled. I froze! "Who's there!?!" I yelled. No one answered. It must have been the wind. But without warning a dark figure staggered out of the bushes. It stepped under the blinking lamp. A man. He lunged at me, pushing me to the floor. He forced himself onto me. I could feel his icy breath against my cheek. He crushed me against the freezing concrete. I tried to push him off but he was too strong. His pig like body squashed my chest. With the little breathe I had left, I screamed as loud as I could. But he covered my mouth and whispered "shhh!" "You'll enjoy this!"

He shredded my clothes with his claws. He stroked my hair. Kissing me hard on my neck. I bit his hand and yelled "Help!" He slapped me and murmured., "Quiet". I felt sick as his cold fingers touched my face and throat. My courage to fight began to slip away. I found myself begging him to stop. But he didn't. "You wanted this didn't you." He breathed, almost smiling. Rain and tears ran down my cheeks. Thunder roared with laughter. Mocking me.

Just as I was giving up, hoping he would be merciful enough to kill me when he was finished; I could see something running towards us. His copper hands clenched into fists. "Get off her, you bastard!" He hollered, his husky voice burning with anger. He dragged the creature off me. Then pounced on him. His fist pulled back and whacked the monster's face.

I curled up into a ball. My clothes were torn and scattered all over the sidewalk. I buried my head into my knees and hugged my legs. The cold rain drizzled down my back. I could hear the fight as more tears stung the back of my eyes, threatening to appear. I didn't want to look up. I didn't want to see *his* face again. Thud! Two seconds of silence followed. It was broken up by footsteps walking towards me. Crunching the frosty grass. I slowly lifted my head. Shivering.

Jason stood in front of me. He took off his coat and dumped it beside me. My heart pounded harder. What was he going to do? Then he pulled his shirt over his head and revealed the upper part of his muscular body. He moved and kneeled down behind me. He lifted up my arms and slotted them into the black sleeves and yanked the t-shirt down. After wrapping me up in his red coat he put his copper arms around me and hugged me tight. "He will burn in hell!" He mumbled.

He lifted my head and gazed into my blue eyes as he asked sympathetically, "You ok, Britt?" I opened my mouth but nothing came out. Jason scooped me up and carried me home. His nose was bleeding and his right eye was black and blue. His dark normally spiky hair was drenched and flattened, two pieces of grass matted in. His bottom lip was split. Dried blood stained his chin. Rain dripped off his forehead and onto me. I pressed my face into his olive chest.

The heavy oak door squeaked as it swung open and my mom peered out. Her anxious face said everything, she blamed Jason. "What did you do to my daughter!?" She exclaimed. Jason brushed past her and carried me through the hallway and into the living room. He laid me on my brown leather sofa than ran upstairs to my bedroom and brought down my fluffy blue blanket. His warm hands pulled the blanket over me. His soft voice comforted me as he gently whispered, "Your safe now, Britt" "Nothing's gonna hurt you!" He leaned over. His lips were a few inches from my forehead, but he pulled away.
    "Jason, I asked you a question!" My mom snarled. She stood in the doorway of the living room with her arms folded tightly against her chest. Jason let go of my hand as he slowly walked over to her. "Jason, what did you do to my daughter?" My mom asked again, scowling. She tried to speak quietly so I couldn't hear.
    His tongue flicked out to moisten his lips. He looked down for a moment and ruffled his hair. He shook his head as if he was unsure what to say. Then he looked back up at her. He took a slow breathe. "Britt, was raped." His voice was rough and croaky. My mom looked devastated. "Where were you!" She asked Jace. "I was going to Eliot's house." Jason replied.

" I was raped!" The words rang in my head. I dissolved into tears as my mom and Jason argued. Immediately Jason stopped yelling and turned around. I scrambled to my feet pushing the blanket off me and ran over to him. He squeezed me tight. I didn't want him to let go.

" I think you should leave!" My mom glared, grinding her teeth. Jason slowly pulled away.

"I'll see you later, Britt." He whispered. He stormed past my mom and slammed the front door. My mom melted from anger into fake tears.

"My poor, baby!" She said as she stretched out her arms. She squeezed me as her short blonde hair wafted in my face. "Now, you lay back down on the sofa and I'll get you some water!" She guided me to the couch.

As I laid on my back, I stared at the moon which was trying to shine passed the dark clouds. Rain tapped on the oak framed window. Thunder banged like drums. My mom walked into the living room. She stood in front of the sofa. Tears drizzled down her pasty face. She distressingly shook a glass of water in her right hand. The ice hit the sides like bells ringing. She placed it on the mahogany coffee table. "I've called the police and their coming to ask you a few questions." She said as she grabbed my hand and kneeled beside me. "They'll get the creep who did this to you!"

"They might need Jason since he was there." "They said you're not allowed to have a shower until they say it's ok to!" "They'll be here soon but in the meantime I have to pick your little sister up from soccer at that other school." "What's it called, that one that's about five miles away from yours?"

"Wilson," I whispered faintly.

"Yeah, that's right!" "Wilson." "You've been through a lot tonight, why don' you try to get some rest before the police get here!" She said, grabbing her grey jacket.

I ignored her, sipping my water.

Immediately after she shut the door, I bolted up to my room. I felt disgusting and dirty. I desperately wanted to take a shower; to wash away my sickening feeling. Wash away everything that had happened. Instead I flopped myself on my double bed and cried into my blue pillow. Powerless. Weak. Worthless....and Alone.

The screeching sound of my window opening, sent chills down my spine. I opened my eyes to see the centre of the pillow. I wished it would swallow me whole and I would be safe in amongst a blue fluffy world. The floor boards under my carpet creaked as someone made their way across the room. It must have been *him*! *He* must have followed us! And now *he's* here in my room! The chills increased.

A small spark of hope was lit inside of me, that maybe he didn't see me laying on my bed. I tried desperately to stop breathing so hard; so that I could keep it that way. But fear had taken over my body and I could no longer control it. My heart beat faster and my breathing became more intensive as the footsteps got louder.

I let out a high pitched squeal as I felt something touch me. Someone or something began to role me over. "Let go of me!" I cried as my limbs flung everywhere like jelly; Hoping that I would hit something. "Brittany..Britt it's me.." A voice said. It sounded familiar but I continued to lash out. "Ouch!" The mysterious object cried. My bed side lamp flicked on and a glimmer of light crumbled away the darkness. Jason sat next to the lamp clutching his nose.

"I thought you were him." I blubbered.

'Aww Britt..I didn't mean to scare you." He whispered, hugging me. The mattress went down as he sat next to me. "I saw your mom drive off and thought you would want company."

"I do." I murmured, staring at the floor. "My mom said that the police will be coming soon to ask some questions."

"Should I leave now, then?" He asked, standing up.

"No!" Panicking, I grabbed his hand. He glanced at his hand then at me.

Instantly, I let go and crossed my arms. Staring at the wall, I whispered dryly. "I don't want to be left alone."

Jace sat back down next to me. "I wont let you be alone." The room was silent for two seconds. "Damn, I should have walked home with you."

"This isn't your fault." I whispered.

Jace looked away, his eyes narrowing. I could feel the anger radiate from him. "I should have killed him when I had the chance." He breathed to himself. I winced.

His eyes flicked to me. Shivering, I hugged myself. The cold I felt wasn't from the temperature of the room. He slowly moved his hands to my face and wiped away my tears with his thumbs. Then he pulled me towards him. Tightly grasping me against his chest. He had replaced his black

t-shirt, that I was now wearing, with a grey one. It felt soft against my cheek. My cold, tear stained cheek.

CHAPTER 2

Knock, knock, knock! My bedroom shook as someone banged on the front door.

"What was that?" I winced as terrifying thoughts filled my head. It could be him! I couldn't answer the door if it was him!

"Open up, this is the police!" A man yelled. Jason began to get up, but I pulled him back down.

"Don't go, Jace!" I begged, shaking my head.

"I'm not leaving you, I'm just getting the door." "It's the police."

"What if it's not, what if it's him?"

"Brittany, trust me!" "It's not!" He stood again, holding out his hand.

I stared at it for a moment. Swallowing hard, I placed mine on his.

As Jason twisted the brass door knob something inside me said stop! Don't do it! My stomach tightened and my heart began to race again. I was about to stop him but it was too late. Jason's face evaporated into pure terror. He drastically tried to close the door. But the creature pushed hard against it. He yanked himself though and tossed Jace to the floor. He sat on top of him and pinned him down; so that he couldn't move. The beast slowly raised his head. "Hello, sweet-art!" He smirked as his green eyes glistened eerily.

I froze in the arms of the banister.

"Run, Britt!" Jace yelled.

"Shut up, you!" The creature spat. Punching him in the face. Jace's right cheek went red. "That's for earlier!" The beast roared.

Jace recklessly jerked about to brake free. Another swing and his left cheek was scratched up. "The more ya move the faster I'm gonna be done with ya and on to finish ya friend!" He smirked.
"Don't you touch her!" Jace scolded as hatred blazed from his eyes. "Britt, get out of here!" Jace yelled. I couldn't! I couldn't move at all! I felt as if my body had been frozen to that spot. Like a deer that stands, staring at an oncoming car.
"I thought I told ya to shut up!" The man roared again as he slapped Jace. Finally, he was capable of freeing his right arm. He slammed his knuckles directly into the demon's nose. He gripped his throbbing nose. Jace backed up his legs and kicked the beast off. He smacked into the front door. It closed with a bang, which made the whole house tremble.
Jace bounced up. He grabbed me and pulled me up the stairs. The animal stumbled to his feet and bounded after us. I dragged behind a little. Unable to make my feet move fast enough. The beast's claws were digging into my heels. I could feel his cold beer breath on my neck. He violently snatched my foot and hauled me back down. Jace watched, panicking, as I fell to the spread out talons of the vulture. He leaped from the top step. Crashing into the beast. We all tumbled down the stairs.
The beast laid on the floor clutching my foot. He dragged his heavy body onto me. His eyes glared red. At that moment, Jason picked himself up. He attacked the unsuspecting beast. He pushed him to the floor. Bracing him down as he raised his arm. The brute caught Jace's fist with inhuman like speed. In a couple of seconds the creature became dominant over Jace.

He flung him across the hallway, with great force. He slammed him into the wall. Then into another. Throwing him around like a ragdoll. I could only watch, rigid by the stairs.
Finally weak and pathetic Jace laid on the cold blooded tiles. The beast leaned over him. His giant shadow casted

over, swamping Jace with darkness. The beast reached down to his pocket. Slowly and carefully he pulled out something sharp. I couldn't see the object at first. It was covered up by his claws. The tip of the object glimmered in the light. After wiping it with his shirt, the beast revealed the object.

It was a dagger! He held it to Jace's throat. Jace swallowed hard. His eyes ached with both fear and hatred. His jaw tightened, but there was nothing he could do.

"Let's finish this, boy!" The bear roared.

Jace shook with fright. I could tell he was trying to keep it under control. But the beast could already see how scared he really was.

"Where should we start?" He spat, relishing his power. "Maybe I'll slice your neck into shreds!" He snarled. "But that won't be no fun, will it!" "I could start with something every young boy treasures!" He smirked as he lowered the knife down Jace's body. Jace clamped his eyes shut and turned his head away. "Or maybe I could slit your stomach, so that you are barley alive when I kill off your little friend." He lifted his arm so that the tip of the knife pointed at me. I froze. Weak. Defenseless. Powerless. But I fought them all off, wanting to do something. I had to do something. Anything!

A sudden surge of adrenaline pumped through me. I leaped into the beast. I sat on top of him, fighting for the dagger. It slowly pointed at my throat. The spiky head twinkled in the hallway light. I tried to point it at the beast. His strength tipped the dagger back at me. Our hands squeezed around it. In a matter of seconds I managed to force the dagger into the creature's paw. Blood trickled down his wrist.

"ahhhh!" He howled. He dropped it onto the floor. He turned all his attention on his hand. Jace and me eyed the dagger. It bounced up and down, until it laid still on the ground. Suddenly all three of us had our eyes on it. Jace was able to get to it before the beast. He threw it into the kitchen and the creature followed.

Now free, Jason pushed me up the first couple of stairs. He glanced over his shoulder. We could just see into the kitchen. The brute was beginning to pick up the knife. "Faster, Britt, faster!" He said as he pushed harder!

"Grrr!" The monster roared

We made it to my room. At high-speed Jace slammed the door in the fiend's face. He backed up in pursuit of keeping the door closed. The beast rammed into it, from the other side. Jace exerted all his strength. He struggled to compete with the full force of the creature. "Lock it, lock it!" He screeched his voice breaking in two places.

"It needs to be locked with a key !"

"Get it!"

"I don't know where it is?" I said running around the room.

"Find it... hurry!" He yelled anxiously.

I swiped the key from my draw. Ran back over to Jace, who was spread out against the door. My hand quivered as I led the key into the slot.

"The key wont turn!" "The door needs to be completely shut!"

"I'm working on it!" Jace said; Wrestling with the door. I tried to help him by leaning against it. The creature howled and bellowed. My heart echoed in my head.

Bang, shut, lock! For a split second we stared, relieved at the white door. With a roar from the beast, we were reminded about the horrors on the other side. The door knob rattled, vigorously. I grabbed Jace. I could hear his heart raging out of his chest. The door was angry. It wanted to force open it's mouth and gobble us up. My grip of Jace tightened. Pounding echoed throughout my room. He held me close. Sweat trickled down his forehead.

"I'm gonna kill ya'll!" The demon threatened; banging against the door.

Suddenly, the house fell silent. The only sounds left were the gasping of Jace and me. Safe at last. Our grateful bodies collapsed onto the floor, with a thud. We sat quietly next to each other, against my bed. Waiting, listening for any sound that meant he was still there. "Do you think he's gone?" Jace whispered, panting.

"I don't know!" I replied. My voice was barely audible.

"I'm gonna find out!" Jace breathed, slowly getting up.

His baggy black jeans flapped as he quietly moved to the door. He sluggishly raised his hand over the handle. Without warning, the doorknob shuddered. Jace went stiff. Keys chimed from the other side. I crawled over to Jace and groped his arm. The monster must have found the spare bunch of keys in the kitchen.

Clink, clank! The keys rustled in the slot; Being turned! I grabbed Jace's hand. We dashed over, to hide behind the other side of my bed. Taking cover, we watched the door. Focused on the knob, I could see it chattering. The door opened. We ducked down under the bed. A classy black shoe appeared. Then another.

The feet walked up and down the side of my bed. I glanced at Jace, who was laying on his stomach beside me. Suddenly, the feet stopped. A knot twisted in my throat as the creature began to kneel down. I bit my lip and shut my eyes.

"Brittany!?!" A familiar voice said, surprised. "What are you and Jace doing under the bed?" Joe asked, concerned.

I opened my eyes; "Where is he?" I asked, getting out from under the bed. Joe's light brown hair was neatly combed forward. The sides trimmed. He was dressed in a tweed grey suit. His white dog collar proudly tucked around his neck. He must have just gotten back from preaching at his convention thing...that he got up early this morning to go to.

"Where's who?" He asked, raising an eyebrow above his round black glasses.

"That man?" Jace added as I helped him up. "Didn't you see him?"

Joe ignored him. "Why are you wearing one of his shirts?" He stared disgusted. I looked down at Jace's black t-shirt.

"Because I'm not allowed to take it off until the police get here!" I replied.

Angered by his judgmental tone.

"What?"

"Oh forget it" "You don't care anyway, Joe" I snapped.

"Well, I do care if my daughter is ..."

"Your daughter!" I interrupted. " I'm not your daughter!" "I had a dad and your not him!" "Your nothing like him!"

"And how would you know!" Joe yelled. "You were about five when he died!"

"I was nine!" I screamed as I stormed out of my room and slammed the door.

I pressed my back against the white hallway wall. Tilting my head, to stare at the ceiling. I covered my face with my hands and slid down. I wanted my dad so bad. This was beginning to feel just like the first month after he had died.

I could hear Jace and Joe. I forced myself not to cry. 'If I can hear them they must be able to hear me.' I thought to myself.

" What are you looking at?" Joe snapped.
"Nothin!" Jace blurted, startled.
"You stay away from her!" Joe threatened.
" What?" Jace huffed, confused.
"You heard me!" Joe shouted. "Don't go near her!" "Don't... don't, talk to her, and most of all don't touch her!"
"Touch her!?!" Jace questioned.
"Yes, I know what your intentions are!"
"Oh I'm sorry.. my... *intentions* !?!" Jace sniggered. I could hear a sarcastic smile in his voice.
"Yes, I was a young lad once!" " There's just *one* thing you want with my daughter!"
"Oh is that true?"
"Yes!"
" And what exactly do I want with, apparently, your daughter!"
" What is that suppose to mean and you know what I'm talking about!"
"She just told you, she's not your daughter!"
"Shut up, you illegal alien!"
"Excuse me!" Jace shouted, disgusted.
"You heard me, Mexican!"
"You went too far and I'm... half... Mexican... just so you know!"
"Oh I'm sorry!" Joe said sarcastically. "I'd rather my daughter didn't sleep with a filthy half Mexican!"

Footsteps charged towards the door. I jumped as it opened. Jace stepped out. His fists clenched. He leaned against the wall. His palms flattened as he took a slow breath. He continued to walk down the hall. Suddenly he stopped. My legs were pinned against my chest. I was a meter from my bedroom door. It was still open. About a crack. I heard a muffling hum. It sounded like Joe was praying. Jace turned. His eyes stared at me. He tilted his head slightly and raised an eyebrow. A tear trickled down my cheek. His face sunk. He moved closer and sat next to me.

My heart shuddered as the doorbell rang. I clenched Jace's arm. My bedroom door flew the rest of the way open and Joe speeded down the stairs and towards the door, without even noticing me and Jace on the floor.

"Hello, this is investigator Paulman and I'm investigator Andrews." A local, Arizonian, accent announced from down stairs. "Umm, is Brittany Chapman here?"

"Yes she is!" "Brittany!" Joe called.

I firmly griped Jace's hand and yanked him down stairs with me. "Maybe you officers will be more comfortable in the sitting room!" Joe said, wailing his arms in the direction of the living room.

"Yeah, thanks!" Inspector Andrews said, leading the way.

I sat tense on the sofa; twiddling my thumbs. "What exactly is this about?" Joe asked, raising his English accent above the sound of inspector Paulman scribbling in his notebook. Andrews and Paulman glanced at each other then at Joe. "Why don't you come with me Mr. Chapman." Andrews said. Joe straightened his white dog collar. Then walked out of the room behind her. "Should we begin then?" Paulman asked. He glanced at us for a second then back down at his notebook.

After I told him what had happened I could feel my whole body shaking. The salty taste of tears lingered in my mouth. "I'm sorry, would you like a break?" Paulman asked. Jace gently held my hand and scooted closer. I tried desperately to stop myself from crying. I didn't want to weep in front of the inspector. But it was no use; I erupted into tears in Jace's arms.

Yelling exploded from the hallway. "What? I can't believe this!" That was Joe's voice.

"Calm down, that's why we're here to get him."

"Don't you tell me to calm down!" I tried to block out the shouting. Jace rubbed my shoulder. Andrews appeared again, sitting on the opposite sofa. Next to Paulman. She looked at his notebook, to see what questions he'd already asked me I guess.

"Do you mind if we ask you some questions?" Andrews queried Jace.

"Yeah, sure." Jace replied, not really paying much attention to what she was saying.

"You saved Brittany, but how did you know she needed help?"

"I was on my way to my friend's house when I heard screaming that sounded like Brittany." Jace answered.

"What's your friend's name?"

"Elliot Gardner."

"OK, and can you describe the man for us?" At that moment a crow tapped on the window. The droplets of water on it's feathers glistened as it squawked.

"Shoo!" Inspector Andrews waved. The crow's red eyes burned as it glanced at me, then flew off.

"His hair was so short that he was almost bald, like stubbly orange hair" Jace began. "He was about fifty years old and about average height." "He had green eyes and an oval face and he was a white dude."

"What was he wearing?"

"He was wearing ripped blue jeans and a dirty white tank shirt."

"Did he have any distinctive features?"

"Like what?" Jace asked

"Like a scar or birth mark?"

"Yeah, he had a scar below his right eye!" Jace said as he fingered his cheek. My throat tightened. Thinking about it, seeing him in my head made me want to throw up. But I stopped myself. Swallowing hard. Fighting against it.

" Ok, well that's enough questions for now!" Andrews said as she stood up.

Before the detectives left they informed Joe that he should take me to the hospital to get a rape kit. He grabbed his keys. "I want Jason to come with me." I said.
He glared at him. Jace glanced at his watch. "My dad's coming home soon." He mumbled. "Please Jace, you promised you wouldn't leave me."
His brown eyes reflected my pain. "Okay." He whispered. Joe grunted as he walked out the door.
I sat on the edge of the examining table. A blanket wrapped around me. The hospital gown was making my skin itch. The nurse had put Jace's shirt into a bag. She left the room to find the Doctor. I felt someone's eyes on me. I lifted my head. Jace was watching me from the other side of the room, where they were told to sit and wait. "Only if your quiet." The nurse said. But Joe asked her too many questions and was thrown out to sit in the waiting room.
Jace got up from the plastic blue chair and walked over to me. He pulled himself up onto the table and sat beside me. "Do you want something to drink?" he asked. I shook my head, then let it fall back down. A fly crawled along the blue lino flooring. It cleaned it's wings with it's front legs, then flew over to the window. The nurse had pulled the curtains shut. I was thankful for that. The night had gotten darker. I wasn't scared of the dark, just what might be out there.

I jumped when the Doctor walked in. It made me feel a little better that Jace did too. "I'm Dr. Heckerman. How are you feeling." Jace narrowed his eyes slightly. As if saying *"What do you think!"*.
"Okay." I said trying to force a smile. I cleared my throat but my voice still sounded distorted. "Can I go home now?" I wanted to take a shower. Wash away everything that had happened.
"In a little while...let's have a look at your bruises first." Jace felt that that was his queue to go sit back down on the blue chair.

The Doctor looked into my eyes with a small light and explained as he went along. He combed through my hair and put the strands into a small plastic bag. Testing and photographing my bruising. After collecting evidence I was finally allowed to go home. Jace did too. His dad's black pick up truck was in the drive way. He seemed scared to go into his house; But I was probably just imaging things.

Pulling off the hospital robe, I stared down at the white tiles. The mechanic was suppose to fix the shower handles. He didn't. My frail hands hopelessly attempted to twist the tap. Weak and worthless, I threw myself onto the floor. My spine touched the cold glass. I sat there for ages, it seems. It didn't matter that the taps were stuck because my tears flooded the room.

The towels on the rack couldn't escape. They tried to swim but drowned in my sorrows. My tears rose up in a wave and turned on the sink. The two liquids merged together. They danced with each other in the ocean, I had created. Suddenly, round and round they turned. In a funnel they swirled and curled, until every drop had fallen down the shower drain.

I had scrubbed so hard that my skin burned. It didn't matter how hard I did, though. I still felt dirty. My arms were purple and now had a tinge of red. I stumbled over to the wide mirror hanging above the sink. A blank face stared back. She was a girl I'd never seen before. No expression. Emotionless. But still my heart went out to her. Her cheeks were covered in bruises and her lips were dry and chapped. Her hair was matted and dripping.

CHAPTER 3

My bedroom didn't feel as safe as it use to. I pushed the covers off and flicked on the light switch. The monsters that survived in the dark ran and hid but threatened to reappear. They planned their revenge in the shadows of my room.

I looked over my shoulder as I sat restlessly at my desk. I stared at my photos on the wall. Three of my favorites were enclosed in black picture frames, a vertical line on my wall.

The first picture was of me and Jace at Elliot's 12th birthday party. Jace and I were still eleven. We're a few months younger then Elliot. I'm the youngest of the three. All of us had smiles that reached from one ear to the other. Spotted party hats stood proudly on our heads. But our eyes hid bruised and battered secrets. Secrets that only the one who kept them, knew about. At that moment I didn't know that Jace and Elliot didn't always tell me everything.

The second picture was of my dad. He was dressed in his army uniform. I use to cuddled it in the months after he passed away. Never taking it out of it's frame because I didn't want it to get ruined. And the bottom photo was of me and Jace, aged seven. We were sitting on a boulder at a beach we went to one year. We had an arm around each other and were grinning.

A tree branch snapped. Was it *him*, attempting to climb the tree, that stood between mine and Jace's window?

Immediately, I twisted my head. I gazed out. I grabbed some scissors; for protection. They shook in my hand. My heart pounded. Outside of my bedroom a darkness smothered the earth. A crow sat at the higher branches, stacking twigs.

More assured that no one was outside, waiting, I pushed up the window. The light was on in Jace's bedroom. Through the branches of the trees I could see him playing his guitar. I grabbed an old pen and threw it. He slowly put down his guitar and looked at me. I signaled him to come over. He opened his window and climbed across.

"What!" "Are you ok!" He asked worried, swinging his legs through.

"No... I can't sleep!" I muttered, feeling my hands shaking at my sides. "Every time I shut my eyes, I have to open them again!" He kept his back to me as he pulled the window down and locked it. "I'm scared Jace!" His eyes flicked to mine. He stepped forward probably wanting to comfort me but I flinched.

"How bout I stay with you until you fall asleep!" He suggested, pretending not to have noticed; Placing his hands on my shoulders.

"I don't think I will sleep!" "Every time I shut my eyes I see *his* face!" Tears exploded out of me. Jace hugged me tight.

"Don't leave me Jace!" I grabbed his waist as he pulled away. Almost piercing through his shirt with my nails.

"O-okay, Britt...it's okay" He whispered, stroking my hair. He'd never seen me cry this much before and neither had I. But I was glad he wasn't telling me to 'get a grip', like I was telling myself. "Where do you want me to sleep?"

"I don't have any sleeping bags." I snorted, as I wiped my tears with my purple pajama sleeve. I got into my bed and wrapped my blue quilt around me. "You could...sleep here." I said scooting over to leave a space. Jace looked at me then at the bed, then back up at me.

"Are you sure?" It wasn't like we hadn't slept in the same bed before (when we were seven).

"Please Jace!" I begged, another tear running down my cheek. I didn't want to be alone.

"Okay." He nodded, gently climbing in next to me. I launched over to hug him. He raised his arms, not sure what I was doing. I rested my head on the pillow. Tears still slipped down my cheeks no matter how much I wanted them to stop. He relaxed a little, resting on his elbow and using his other hand to wipe my tears. "Shhh.." He whispered softly as he wrapped his arm around me and pulled me closer. He kissed my forehead. "Don't cry Britt." He soothed. "The windows are locked, the doors are locked and all of your family are here... nothing can hurt you."

"Could you check under the bed?" I sniffed. He half smiled; but I was serious. A gust of wind irritated the tree outside. It's branches scratched at the window. Listening to the moans I knew it was just the wind but I still jumped at the noise. "What was that?" I screeched, sitting up. Jace pulled my shoulders back down and cuddled me in his warm arms. "It's nothing...I'm right here, nothing's gonna get you." He whispered calmly. I couldn't help it. Three more tears escaped, one after the other. "Aww...Britt." He muttered, wiping my eyes.

"I just can't help thinking...that maybe...is this my fault?" I lifted my head to stare guiltily at him.

"No...Brittany no." He breathed into my hair as he gently pecked my forehead again. "This was *not*...completely *not* your fault!"

"But...Jason...*he* said that ..I..I.. wanted it, that I w...was asking for it." I whimpered as more tears flowed down my cheeks. "*He* did what?" Biting down hard on the last word. He shook his head and hugged me tighter. After a moment he released me and wiped another tear from my face.

"Brittany...this is not your fault." "That sick 'Mérida' wants you to feel like it's your fault, but it's not, it's all about power, Britt...he wanted to feel powerful over you!" He murmured through his clenched teeth. His jaw softened. "This is *not* your fault, and don't let anyone tell you anything different." He whispered. Only then did I consider that this wasn't my fault. But that didn't stop me feeling ripped open and frightened. Like a part of me had been torn out.

I wrapped my arms around Jace's shoulders and buried my head into his chest. His arm slid further around me and he gently rubbed my back with his hand. I'd never really smelled Jace before. But as I closed my eyes the scent of a husky aroma with a honey back ground twigged my brain. Did Jace *always* smell of honey? The warmth and smell of Jace helped me slowly drift away.

Suddenly the horrors of the day replayed in my dreams. Tearing them apart and transforming them into nightmares. *His* green eyes stared eerily at me. His beer breath and the smell of fresh rain mixed together. I was there again. Reliving it. A part of my mind clicked. It reminded me that I could open my eyes and this would stop. All I had to do was open them. Panting and sweating , I realized I was crying. Again. It was one of those nightmares where you know all you have to do is open your eyes but you can't. Your trapped.

"Brittany...Brittany...open your eyes ." Someone encouraged. It was Jace's voice. His hands molded to fit my face. "Listen to me...open your eyes." He whispered gently. I could feel the bed shaking as I shivered. "Voy a coutar hasta cinco." (I'm going to count to five.) "Uno, dos, tres, cuatro, cinco." (One two three four five) "Abre los ojos" (Open your eyes) I forced back my eyelids.

He ran his fingers through my hair and kissed my forehead. "Shhh." He comforted. "It's ok..." "Your safe Britt... your safe." His hand slid back down to my back. "Go back to sleep..." He whispered, closing his eyes. "You need to sleep." He whispered again, the sentence trailing off near the end. I snuggled close then shut my eyes and fell asleep as Jace drew on my back.

Jace rubbed his eyes as he stretched. "What time is it?"

I turned over to look at my soccer ball clock on my bedside table. "It's 12.00 o'clock!"

"12:00?" He jumped out of bed. "My Dad's gonna kill me!" "I gotta go!" I grabbed his arm. "Jace wait." I didn't want him to go. Not yet at least. Even just a minute longer. "What does Mérida mean?" I murmured, trying to pronounce it like he did last night. He rolled his eyes as he smiled crookedly. "It means shit, Britt, ...can I go now?" He laughed. I released his arm. He headed towards the window, "See ya later, Britt!"

CHAPTER 4

TWO WEEKS LATER

"Happy Birthday to you, happy birthday to you..." Voices sang to me. I opened my eyes and immediately sat up. My family were gathered around my bed with a birthday cake. "Happy Birthday dear Brittany..."

"Aww, thanks you guys!" I smiled

"Open my present first!" My little sister, Kelly, grinned. She had her brown hair in pigtails. She pushed the gift directly in front of my face. Kelly is actually my half sister. She's eight years old and I swear she's in love with Jace! Her best friend is Shannon, that's Elliot's little sister. Her smile was the only genuine one in the room. The only one who didn't know about 'that night'. Everyone else forced on a smile and pretended it never happened.

"Thanks Kelly!" " Did you talk to Shannon yesterday?"

"Yeah, her and Elliot are still at their Granny's house." She said depressed.

Tearing at the wrapping paper, I continued our conversation. " You know they're coming back later today!"

"They are?!" she jumped around with joy.

After everyone had given their presents they left my room and did their own things, like normal.

Suddenly, something tapped at my window. I swiftly turned to see what it was. Every little sound scared me, now. It was Jace. I jumped up and unlocked the window.

"Thanks!" He smiled. He was holding a red package. Clambering through he caught a foot. He fell face first onto the floor. I burst out laughing. He slowly helped himself up.

"You're not suppose to laugh at your friends when they fall on their face!" He scowled.

"Who said you were my friend!?!" I sniggered sarcastically.

"That's it, you don't get your present!"

"I'm sorry Jace." I smiled. "I love you really!"

"That's better!" "Here you go!" He beamed, handing over the gift.

"Happy Sweet Seventeenth!" The label said. I recklessly shredded the wrapping paper.

"Student Lawyer Book." "Thanks Jace!" I smiled happily as I flipped through the pages. "Where did you get it?"

"In a book store." "Now you will know most of the stuff before you get into law school!" He laughed.

Without warning, a putrid green cloud hung over my head.

"Woah!" "Britt, your going pale." I covered my mouth and ran to the bathroom. Jace didn't follow. "Flush!" I walked over to the mirror and wiped my mouth with a flannel. Then rinsed with Listerine for at least a minute. I unlocked the door and slowly walked back into my room. He jumped up from sitting on my bed and stared at me worried.

"Are you ok?"

"Yeah, I'm fine." I lied.

"Are you sure?" Jace paused for a few seconds. "Did you eat this morning?"

"Not yet." What was this, some kind of interrogation.

"Britt?" Jace began to whisper. He stepped closer. "When was your last period?" His almond eyes were serious.

"Do you really need to know that?" I asked, confused.

"When was it?" He insisted.

"I don't know, maybe last month."

His eyes widened, worried. He swallowed and moistened his lips. "Ok!" He said as if he was thinking of the nicest way to tell me something. "Britt, I think.." "I think you might be.."

"I might be what?"

"Pregnant!" He whispered.

"What!" "No, I can't be!" I said in disbelieve. "I mean I could just have a bad flu or something." "And also you need to have sex to become pregnant and I'm a .." I stopped in mid sentence. My mind flashed back to that night. Two weeks ago. I was raped. Tears flowed down my cheeks. "I'm pregnant!"

Jace hugged me "There is a chance you might not be!" He whispered.

"Does your mom or anyone have any tests?"

"I don't think they do." "I'll go look in the cupboard." Jace followed as I walked to the bathroom. We both raided the little white cupboard next to the mirror on the wall. I pulled out a rectangular blue box. *"Quick Stream" "One step pregnancy test."* Jace looked at the box. "I'll be outside if you need anything."

My eyes watched him open the bathroom door. "Jace wait!" I said putting the box down by the sink.

I walked over to him and hugged him, for support. "It'll be fine, Britt!" "You're probably right, you might just have the flu or something."

I put the test down by the sink and washed my hands. I stared at myself in the mirror. "It's probably nothin', Britt." I whispered to myself. I ruffled my hair and closed my eyes. After a few seconds I looked down. There it was. In the little square, was that color. Blue. I was pregnant! I could feel tears wrenching through. I slowly opened the white bathroom door. Jace stood up from the floor. His eyes sympathetic. He pulled me towards him and hugged me tight. "What am I goin' to do with a baby?" I sobbed. "How am I gonna be a lawyer now?"

"I know what your goin' to say but..."

"But what?"

"I think you should have an abortion!" I pushed him away and stepped back.

"What?" "Jace I can't murder this baby!" I snapped, raising my voice.

"That's what I thought you'd say." He mumbled, mostly to himself.

"Yeah well, I'm a Catholic and you know we believe that's wrong!" Jace pulled me back into my room and closed the door.
"You can't keep it!" Jace began to raise his voice, too.
"I have to!"
"Britt you can't keep this *thing*!"
"It's not a thing it's a living being!"
"That living thing is gonna ruin your life, Britt!"
"I can't kill it!"
"Do you know how painful giving birth is?" He asked.

"No!"
"Well me neither, but I've seen some of those obstetrician shows with Elliot and those women are screaming pretty loud!" Before I could ask he included, "He's thinking about being a doctor." He half-smiled.
"I don't care you can't make me kill a living thing!"
"It can't even breathe, technically it's not living!"
"I can't believe your saying this!" I yelled.
"I can't believe *your* saying this!" He yelled back. "Britt, that jackass got you pregnant!" "Your gonna have to go through labor and throwing up every morning …" Jace paused for a few seconds. He lowered his voice; "I don't wanna watch you suffer because of him!"

I looked away. Then at the floor and ran my fingers through my blonde hair. A tear ran down my cheek as I whispered, "Then don't!"
Jace stared at me bewildered. "Britt.."
"Just go, Jace!" I snapped. He slowly moved over to the window and left, only looking back once.
I collapsed in the middle of my room, clawing the cream carpet.
What am I going to do? Please God help me.
At that moment I remembered my secret was still laying in the bathroom. I ran through and picked up the pregnancy test off the sink. I stared at it as I walked into the hallway

hoping that somehow it would change to a different color any other color but blue. Or maybe, just maybe, it was just the bathroom lighting.

"What's that?" I froze. I looked up to see the disappointed face of my mother.

"It's nothing!" I knew she wasn't that stupid but what else could I say.

"It doesn't look like nothin!" I attempted to hide it behind my back ,but she managed to catch my hand. She stared at it for a few seconds. Maybe she thought that her eyes were deceiving her. "Brittany, it's blue!" She said in shock.

She grabbed my hand and dragged me into my room. "Sit there!" She said, pointing to my bed; before I could say anything.

"Are you pregnant?" She asked, her hands on her hips. I felt like she was standing over me. Suffocating me. I didn't want to cry. I was stronger than that. I knew crying wouldn't make anything better; But one tear escaped. I wiped it away with my blue sleeve as I confessed. "Yes!" I bit my lip. She stumbled slightly as if she was going to faint. Her face turned paler then normal.

"Oh Brittany." She sighed as she sat next to me. Her hands slid over her face. "Who's is it?" She asked, muffled. "What?" I was confused. Who's did she think it was? She lifted her head. "Please don't tell me it's Jason's." She frowned.

"Jace?" I repeated, unsure I heard her correctly.

"Is that a yes?" She asked surprised, straightening her back. Once again, she had fixed it in her head that Jace was to blame. "Does he know?" "Does his dad know?" "Is he going to support you?" She stood before I could answer any of her questions. "Oh my goodness, I can't believe he did this to you." She whispered, crossing her arms.

My eyes followed her as she walked up to the window. "Jason!" She yelled loudly. I couldn't see out of it that well, from my bed. I heard the tree branches rustling. Jason climbed through. She scowled at him.

"Yes!?!" He asked, rudely. She waved the test in the air. His face sunk. He glanced over at me for a split second.

"Brittany has told me everything!" She announced. "She told me it's your baby." My mouth dropped. Lie! I yelled in my head; so loud that my ears rang. Jace's dark eyebrows scrunched together.

"What?" He asked confused. He glanced at me. "You told her this was my baby?"

I couldn't get anything to come out of my mouth. I unsteadily shook my head. My mom placed her hands on her hips. "Yes you did." She frowned.

"Brittany why would you tell your mom that I got you pregnant?" Jace asked, still confused. I sensed a hint of anger in his voice. He was mad at me. Mad because of my mom's lie. All I had to do to put it right was say something. Anything. But I couldn't talk. My throat dried.

I shook my head again and stood. "Maybe she said it because it's the truth!" Hilary scowled. "You haven't denied it after all."

"Well it's a lie!"

"Prove it!"

"Ok.." He nodded. Pausing, he glanced at the floor and moistened his lips to think of something. "It's pretty obvious Hilary, that it was that asshole who raped her!"

"It's too early..." Her sentence drained out. She shook her head. "I know that you climb through her window, Jace." I can remember when we were twelve and my mom thought we were getting too old to climb through each others windows.

Jace continued to climb through my window anyway. He said he liked the company.

For a few seconds Jace looked a little stunned. He probably thought that she didn't know that he was still climbing through my window at night. I wasn't that surprised, she seemed like she knew something. "What does that have to do with this?" Jace asked.

"You've been sneaking into her room every night since ya'll were seven. It has to be yours."

Jace's eyes narrowed. "That doesn't mean anything!"

"Doesn't it?"

"I've never slept with Brittany!" He rose his voice.

"You still haven't proven that to me."

He threw his hands in the air and groaned, frustrated. "I don't have any proof, okay."

"Then it has to be your baby."

"Like I said before, it was the asshole..." Jace didn't finish his sentence. I seemed to have caught his eye and he stopped talking.

He turned his back to my mom and walked towards me. He sat down next to me, on my bed. Then slowly raised his copper arm and pushed back a piece of blonde hair out of my face. "I'm sorry!" he whispered. He glanced down at the floor for a split second then continued.

"I'll support you with whatever you choose!" "Because that's what friends do!"

"Thanks Jace." I sniffed.

"Wait, are you keeping the baby?" She asked. I nodded. "Brittany." she whispered, kneeling in front of me. Her pale hand placed on mine. "You can't have this baby."

"What?" I mouthed. I couldn't believe she was saying this. Wasn't this my catholic mom? Wasn't this the woman who had told me on many occasions that abortion was evil? Was she telling me to forget my morals; to forget hers? "Sweetie." She breathed sitting between me and Jace. "What will people say when you can no longer hide it?" She squeezed my hand. "Joe's reputation will be ruined." "Can you understand what I'm saying?" I didn't. How could I? I glanced at Jace. He was glaring at the floor. His fists resting on his knees.

"You mean an abortion?" I mumbled, knowing the answer.

"Yes dear." She whispered. "I'm sure no one will disapprove under the circumstances." I pulled my hand out of her grasp and cradled it with the other. Staring at the orange paint stain on the floor. "Honey, think about how this'll effect Joe... how will it look if a priest's step daughter is pregnant?..w.. what will people say?" "Think about that, and your little sister..she'll get called names!"

The bed bounced slightly underneath me, as Jace stood up. He crossed his arms. "And what about Brittany?" He yelled.

"I beg your pardon?" Hilary scoffed , shocked.

"Think who's the one who is pregnant here." "The one who was raped!" "What about her!...She'll be called names too... and what about her reputation, 'Look at her..it's the straight A school girl who was stupid enough to get knocked up'!" "You think she wants that?" "You think that even though she says she doesn't care what people think, deep down she wont be hurting?"

Hilary couldn't speak after Jace's protest. A minute after, she realized her jaw had dropped and she pulled it back up. She crossed her arms and stormed out. Taking her pride, I guess she thought that it was beneath her to argue with Jace. Why, I wasn't sure.

I leaned over my windowsill and gazed outside. The black crow was still there. I could just make out that the pile of sticks was the bottom of a nest. Jason pushed in next to me. I glanced at him. He was staring out the window. "Do you wanna watch a movie?" he asked, smiling.

"Sure!" I said, reaching out to him. He hugged me.

"What do you want to see?" He asked as he lightly hit my arm.

"I don't care!" I said, punching him back.

"Ow!" He winced, grabbing his arm. His bright eyes converted into pain. For a second he glanced at me. Shaking it off as if it was nothing.

"I'm sorry!" "Are you ok!"

"Yeah.. it's nothin!" He blurted out, as if he was trying to hide something.

"Let me see." I pulled up his long grey sleeve. He flinched but allowed me to continue, he knew that I never let things go. He always said that that's why I'd make a good lawyer, never giving up. His olive arm was purple and black with blotches of cigarette burns.

"What happened?" I asked, astonished.

He didn't answer.

"Jace!?!"
"Nothin!"
"It doesn't look like nothin!" I persisted.
"Umm... I fell down the stairs!"
"On some cigarettes?"

Jace stared at the floor and ruffled his hair. This reminded me of other bruises I'd seen before. He'd started getting them when he was ten, after his mom died.

"Jace, you've been falling down the stairs for seven years now." I ridiculed. "Was it your dad?"

His eyes narrowed. "Why do you always think that when I get a bruise or a cut or something that it was my dad?" He defended.

"I've seen how your dad gets when he's angry or drunk!"
"That doesn't mean that he hits me!"
"Are you sure?"
"I don't wanna talk about it!" He whispered, staring at the floor.

"Was he drunk or something?"

"Britt please, just drop it!" He begged, his eyes glancing back up for half a second. He trudged over to my bed and put his head in his hands. I squatted in front of him and gently placed my hands on his knees.

"Does your dad physically abuse you, Jason?" I whispered, trying to connected with his eyes. He glanced at me then back at the floor. Shoving his tongue into his cheek he bit down. "Jason you can tell me!"

Finally he looked straight up and nodded.

"Jace.."

"You can't tell anyone!" He interrupted; His voice was rough and croaky as if he had a lump in his throat.

"Jason you need to tell someone.."

"Brittany no!" He interrupted again. "No one can know!"

"Jace your dad beats you!" "You need to tell social services!" I informed. "I'll even call them for you!" I began to get up but Jace caught my hands.

"Brittany, listen to me!" He whispered, leaning in. "If my dad gets arrested I have to go with child services!" "I don't want that!"

"So you'd rather be your dad's punching bag!?" I argued. "Jason, they can take him away and you'll never have to see him again!"

"Exactly.." He paused for a second. "He's still my dad, Britt!"

His grip of me slowly slipped away. I stood up and held him close. I felt him squeeze me back.

Jace needed some cheering up; I sat next to him on the bed. "So what movie are we going to see?" I said nudging his shoulder with mine. Trying to brighten the atmosphere. It worked. I found it easy to make him smile.

"I hear there's supposed to be cake on people's birthdays!"

"It's downstairs!" I smirked, rolling my eyes. "Do you ever think of anything other then food?"

"Yeah, sleeping." He laughed as he ran to the door.

Standing by the kitchen table with a big milk mustache, and a slice of cake on a pink plastic plate, was Kelly. She smiled widely at Jace. "Hi Jason!"

"Hey Kelly!" He smiled. I elbowed him. "You got a little admirer!" I whispered, in his ear. He looked a little scared but then shrugged. He lowered himself to Kelly's height with a napkin in his hand. "You got something right there!" He giggled, wiping her face. She blushed a little. "Thanks Jace!" "Hey Jason do you like my pigtails?" She asked sweetly, swaying side to side.

"I love your pigtails, Kelly." He said as he tapped her nose. "Tehe!" She giggled.

He stood back up and wrapped his arm around her. "Where's the cake Kells?" "It's over here!" She immediately lead him to the bread box.

"Kelly your not suppose to tell him!" I laughed.

"The man is hungry!" She hissed. Jace winked at me.

He grabbed a napkin from the draw and placed his cake on top. Suspiciously, he drifted towards me. Suddenly he raised up the napkin and smacked the cake into my face. I opened my mouth in shock. He crammed the rest in. He laughed as he ran. I swallowed it, then cut a small slice of my own. "Come here Jason!" I growled. He chuckled cowardly on the opposite side of the breakfast bar. Suddenly, he darted to the circular wooden table, in the middle of the kitchen. I chased him round and round. Finally I slammed him onto the floor; Pinning him down with my legs and left arm. "Mercy.." he chocked through his laughter. " I beg for mercy!" I smothered his face in cake and frosting. "Revenge is sweet!" I giggled, watching him lick his lips.

"Jason, are you ok!" Kelly said running to his side, heroically.

Someone knocked at the front door. "I got it!" Tasha, my older sister, yelled. Footsteps pounded down the stairs. "Hello is Brittany here!" A familiar voice asked.

"Yeah." She said, disappointed. She was probably hoping for Ryan, her boyfriend. "Brittany!" she yelled. I glanced over to Jace. He recognized the voice too.

Investigator Andrews stood in the hallway. "We have a few things to tell you." "Are your parents home?" she asked. At that moment my mom walked through from the living room.

"Mrs. Chapman!" Andrews said raising her hand. "We talked on the phone two weeks ago." My mom shook hands as she glanced at me. "Yes!"

"We need to take Brittany and Jason down to the station."

CHAPTER 5

ELLIOT GARDENER

I stared at the fuzzy television screen; Shannon beside me on the dark blue fabric sofa. We had just scrapped up the exact amount to get it. $80 was a stretch for us, we didn't have a lot of money. The couch wasn't in the best condition. Foam was falling out near the bottom of the left arm. It had a few stains; But it did the job.

Suddenly the box hissed and cursed. Zig zag lines ran down the screen. Grey, white then black. 'Oh great!' I sighed to myself. So the electric was cut too. I glanced at Shannon's disappointed face. "Sorry." I apologized. She smiled; Her nose wrinkling like it normally did when she smiled. "We could do something else!" She said. Putting on a positive spin. Her spirit made me smile back. It was involuntary. Whenever she smiled I had to smile too, like an automatic reaction.

There was nothing else to do. I had already unpacked mine and Shan's bags, from visiting our Granny in Oklahoma (We only see her once or twice a year). She's our mother's mom and has no one else. Shannon doesn't like going. She says she smells like cat food.

"I'm hungry." She muttered, clambering down from the sofa. I wandered into the kitchen, not really expecting there to be any food. There wasn't. Just a box of Cheerio crumbs, off milk in the fridge and a mini Hershey's chocolate bar. I grabbed the chocolate and gave it to Shannon, who halved it. Her brilliant blue eyes beamed as she lifted a half to me. Smiling, I took it and shoved it in my mouth. Licking my lips, I figured Shan would still be hungry too.

I was considering if it was too dark to stop by Britt's when the door bell rang. "Hello?" I answered, opening just enough that my body could fit through. Two men in suits stood patently. The taller one showed me his badge as he said, "Do you know where we can find Elliot Gardener?"

"I'm him.." I said cautiously. They pushed there way in. Managing to turn me around and push me up against the wall. Something cold snapped around my wrists.

CHAPTER 6

INVESTIGATOR GILMAN

I marched to the interrogation room. Walking faster then most people. "Sir." Investigator Paulman drew my attention as he caught up with me. I sipped my coffee not bothering to stop. "Elliot Gardener is in interrogation, Investigator Reena is watching his sister Shannon." He informed.

"Is this the guy who raped Brittany Chapman?" I asked.

"The DNA results say so." He said, handing me the file. "He seems very confused."

"Putting it on I expect...well don't worry I'll crack him." I flipped through the pages. "Does he have a record?"

"Yeah he's been arrested a few times before, but he was only a kid so they let him go."

"What did he do?" I asked.

"Stole items from Wal-Mart...a radio, some diapers and other baby stuff."

"Does he have a fetish for baby things then?"

He shrugged his shoulders.

"I'll find out..this guy might have more on him then we expected."

"So, where's the mother?"

"Elliot said she was at work..should we go and get her?"

"No, no leave her. Have you got anything out of him yet?"

"I didn't start, I thought you might want the honors."

"You know me so well." I smiled, stopping at the door. Fixing my graying hair before I went in.

I expected a man at least nineteen but he was only a boy, seventeen. He sat staring at his hands. His green and brown stripped sweater looked as if he'd owned it for a while. A piece of green thread hung down by his arm. He had orange curly hair and green eyes. "Elliot?" I said, closing the door behind me. He looked up.
"Why am I here?" He asked, puzzled.
"We'll get to that later."
Placing the file on the steel table I sat opposite him. I decided to start off easy on him. Lull him into a false sense of security. "I'm Investigator Gilman." I announced, opening the file.
Slipping out a photo of the victim I laid it flat in front of him. "Do you recognize this girl?"
"Yeah that's Brittany." Elliot stared at the picture. "Is she okay?" He asked glancing up at me.
"Can you tell me her full name, you know... for the record." I asked wanting to be precise.
"Brittany Chapman...she doesn't have a middle name." "What happened...oh my God she's not dead, is she?"
"Calm down...she's alive." "She was raped."
"Raped?" He whispered, lowering his head and pushing his eyebrows together.
"When...Who did it?"
"Don't act like you don't know."

"I don't...wait, you don't think *I* did it?"
"Did you?"
"No!" He defended disgusted.
"DNA found on her says otherwise. Which means you're the father of the fetus too."
"The fetus?"
"She's pregnant."
His jaw dropped.
"No, no she can't be pregnant.."
"Oh yeah, why's that?"
"She's smart, you know...she has a future." He paused for a second. "Pregnant? Are you sure?"

"Does this mess up your plan?" I asked, beginning to apply pressure on him.

His eye's narrowed. "I don't ha..."

"Where were you two weeks ago on November 15th at 6:25?" I interrupted, before he could finish.

"At home."

"Can you be more specific?"

"I asked Jace to come over after school so he could help me pack my bag, that way I could help Shan. We were going to our Granny's. I asked Britt, but she said she had to study... we have a test coming up."

"Can anyone confirm that?"

"What?"

"Was anyone with you."

"My mom was at work and Shannon was at soccer practice."

"So...you have no alibi"

"I didn't do it!"

"See Elliot, that's hard for me to believe cus all the evidence points at you." "What I think is..." I laid down photos of the crime scene as I talked. "You knew Jason and Brittany walked home through the forest everyday after school. You knew that that day they had track and wouldn't be out until 6:00, so you got rid of the competition by asking Jason to meet you at your house."

His jaw clamped shut. He obviously didn't like where this was going.

"You wanted Brittany to yourself. She was wearing those short shorts..." I laid down a picture of the school track uniform. His nostril flared slightly as he flicked his eyes to the picture. "You couldn't help yourself."

I waited a moment or two before he replied. He glared at me. "Did you just now make up that load of crap or did it take time?"

"Oh I'm sorry, did I miss out something...like how you followed her home and tried to kill her."

His eyes widened. "Kill her?"

"Look, it will make it easier on everyone including you if you just confess now. Your looking at life for rape and attempted murder. Confess now and we can get you a deal."

He stayed silent; just scowling at the wall. "Hey, I'm a guy I know how it is. Come on, you loved her...wanted her all to yourself but she didn't love you. You figured if you couldn't have her then no one can.

"What don't you get...I didn't do it!" He yelled slamming his fist on the table.

"So, you don't love her?"

"Yeah I love her, but like a sister."

I turned and smiled at the glass. *'We've got more on him now'* I thought. "You have an eight year old sister." I folded my hands. "Shannon right?"

"Yeah...that doesn't have anything to do with this."

"Maybe...maybe not."

"What?" He mouthed, confused.

At that moment the door squeaked. Both me and Elliot looked over. A little lady dressed in a white blouse with a grey pencil skirt stepped in. Investigator Reena stared at the suspect for a second then scurried over to me. Her brown hair was in a short ponytail. "Someone messed up, down in the lab." She whispered faintly in my ear. "Here...this explains everything." She handed me a piece of paper. As fast as she came in she disappeared.

I read the paper then placed it under the open file. "Tell me about your father, Elliot!"

"My dad?" He queried, crossing his arms. "There's not much to tell."

"Where is he?"

"I wouldn't know!" His voice was angry.

"What do you mean?"

He stared at the floor for a second then leaned in as his eyes narrowed. "He walked out on us when my mom was pregnant with Shannon!" Then he sat back, folded his arms and looked away. "Well, it turns out that your not in as much trouble as you thought you were. Turns out it wasn't your DNA found on Brittany." I admitted shuffling the papers.

"So who was it?" He asked, straightening his back. I was surprised that he didn't say I told you so.

Hoping that this might not be a waist of time I pulled out Elliot's record papers from the file. Maybe we could get *something* on this kid. "Let's talk about the things you've stolen."

He leaned back again. "That was a long time ago."

The paper rustled in my hands. "So...you're a thief."

"*Not* anymore!"

"Looking at this, you mostly stole a bunch of baby stuff. Now why is that?"

"For Shannon."

I didn't fully understand, so I let him continue. Waiting in silence.

Elliot glanced to the wall and cleared his throat. "Okay..." He sighed, looking back at me.

"My mom was always working." He said, slowly. "But every job she had... she either got fired from... or didn't get enough pay." "I had to look after Shannon." "When she was about one...I was ten... we were running out of money..." "So... one day after school I walked to Wal-Mart, headed straight to the toddler section and shoved as much stuff into my backpack as I could."

Suddenly, a tall skinny man with fluffy brown hair entered interrogation. A cardboard box tightly hugged to his chest. "I got a surprise for you." Paulman said.

Elliot sat back and stared at the ceiling. Probably thinking '*how much longer..?*'. Bang! He dumped the box on the table. Elliot jumped. Paulman smiled. "You wont believe this.." He murmured. "You know that unsolved case you were working on a while back?"

"Yeah?"

"Well this case is connected." He opened the box and lifted a photo up. "Maybe Elliot can be of more use to us."

"This is very interesting..." I mumbled reading the paper on top. "Thanks Paulman."

"No problem, sir." He smiled, leaving.

I pulled out a compact file, overflowing with papers. I slipped off the elastic band. It snapped. Elliot eyed the file curiously. Flipping through the pages, I read quietly. Refreshing my memory.

"It was nice of you to tell me about your sister and your dad…now tell me about your brother." I folded my hands. Elliot's eyebrows pulled together. "What?" He asked softly.

"Tell me about your brother." I raised my voice.

"I..I don't have a brother." He said, still confused.

"Nick Gardener." I yelled, slamming my hand on the desk. I had had enough with games. He glanced around the room, as if looking for an answer.

I pushed the photo in front of him. He looked it over. He raised an eyebrow, shaking his head. "Umm a dead guy?"

"That is Nick Gardener twenty years ago after he committed suicide." I said sternly. "Did your dad never tell you, you had a half brother?"

"No."

"So, you don't know anything about this unsolved case?" I softened my voice.

He shook his head.

"Twenty years ago I was assigned a case where these men were smuggling drugs from Mexico. Me and my team had narrowed it down to four people. Your father and your half-brother Nick, but we weren't sure who the other two were. We had been trying to drag your dad down for a while but we got nothing on him."

"Well one day a man came to us and said he'd witnessed a murder that was connected to this case. Brown hair, blue eyes, pretty young fella. His name was Charlie Fairbrother. Does this name ring any bells?"

"Yeah." He sat up. "That's Brittany's dad…but he died when she was nine, killed in action."

"That's right, anyway Nick murdered someone who 'knew too much'. We arrested him and he hung himself in prison. No one knows what happened to your dad…he just disappeared off the map."

"Wait…so what does this have to do with *this* case?" He asked curious.

"The evidence found on Brittany matched your DNA by fifty percent."

He froze. His eyes wide with horror. "What?" He whispered weakly. "No, no but that would mean..." He shook his head, unsteadily. Swallowing hard, he clenched his fists on the table. "My dad?" He asked. I nodded once. He sat back for a minute glaring at the wall. "Damb it, that asshole." He spat. His chair screeched as he stood. Leaning over me. "And you don't know where he is?"

I sensed the anger build inside of him. I would've been scared if I didn't know better. "Now you just calm down."

"Calm down?" He yelled. "You want me to calm down!" He dragged on. Knocking over the chair. Yelling and cursing. I stood up and braced him against the wall. The anger faded and he broke down. "How could he do this?"

"Why...why would he do this? He tried to kill her!" His eyes narrowed. "He...he raped her...my dad, my flesh and blood." I let go and stepped back. He swallowed hard. "I'm fine." He lied, recomposing himself.

I had never been very good at the reassuring thing. Feeling like I wasn't helping, I walked back to the table and stacked the papers. "Thank you for your time, Elliot, I'm sorry about the mix up."

CHAPTER 7

ELLIOT GARDENER

I spotted Jace and Britt in the hall. Britt's eye's were red and blotchy, like she'd been crying. She had her jacket tightly pulled around her; But it wasn't that cold inside. I couldn't take my eyes off her. I don't know why. A door slammed and she jumped. I clamped my jaw shut. This was all *his* fault. Or was it mine? Did I do this to her? If she had come to my house nothing would have happened.

"Elliot!" Brittany called, smiling slightly. She ran towards me. Why was she so happy to see me? Like I deserved that. Jace followed swiftly behind her. "I'm so sorry you had to go through that." She whispered, hugging me. I hugged her back loosely. "This must be the worst birthday ever." I chocked. "Wait…" I pushed her back, gripping her shoulders. "You saw that?"

She nodded weakly.

"Britt, I am so sorry." I whispered, shaking my head. She stared at the floor. I could tell she was trying not to cry; but one tear escaped. I wiped it away with my thumb. Wait a minute, Jason was with her. He could have stopped this. I glared at him. "This is all your fault!" I yelled. Stepping past Brittany.

"I d...didn't d..." He stuttered confused by my sudden burst of anger. To tell you the truth so was I.

"You let her get raped?" I wanted Jace to be my dad, wanted to blame him. He wasn't here, so I had to make do with the nearest person.

"No!"

"You were suppose to protect her!" I was ready for a fight. I wanted him to yell back. Fight back!

"I tried!"

"You didn't do a very good job she's pregnant, Jace!" Both Britt and him flinched at the word. "What did you do... just stand back and watch?" I continued to shout, emphasizing each word with frustration. A few passers by stared, but I didn't care.

"I was going to your house...you asked me to come over, remember?" Jace raised his voice.

"You could have walked her home first...it was dark."

"She said she was fine walking by herself...besides we always walk through that forest."

"Look at her she's tiny...just because nothing jumps out now doesn't mean it wont!" Jace glanced at Britt then back at me.

"Don't blame me! This was your asshole dad. He did this to her, not me."

That didn't help. Instead of getting all my anger out I only got stabbed with a fork. "I know." My voice didn't sound like me. Jace was ready to yell something else but he shut his mouth.

I noticed a faded bruise on Britt's arm. Jace seemed to know what I was thinking. "Most of them are almost gone. They were all over her." I was thankful that he didn't want to punish me further for blaming him. Maybe it was because he blamed himself too. Something on Jace's arm caught my attention. I stepped closer. Pushed up his sleeve and revealed a fresh purple bruise. My eyebrows pulled together, curious.

He abruptly shoved away my arm and stepped back. Pulling his sleeve down.

"What was that?"

"Nothin" He blurted out. Brittany stepped forward and opened her mouth. Jace glared at her. She shut it. "Jace he wont tell anyone." She whispered.

He glanced at me then back at her. Staring at his sleeve, he pulled it back up. He lifted his shirt. His side had red blotches in the shape of fists. "My...dad.." He cleared his throat. "My dad...beats me."

My jaw dropped. He pulled his shirt and sleeve back down. His eyes dark with pain. "Is that why you came to school with a black eye about a month ago?"

"Yeah." He chocked.

At that moment a short man in a grey suit with greasy dark hair stormed out of one of the doors in the hallway. The black door had a bronze notice reading 'Evan's Office'. "I heard yelling, will you keep it down!" The man shouted, frustrated. Jace raised his hands, palms flat. "Sorry, we were just leavin'." I nodded in agreement; but didn't look at Britt as we made our move. I felt weird next to her, knowing what *my* dad had done.

CHAPTER 8

BRITTANY CHAPMAN

Together in a line we wandered down the halls of the police station, looking for the exit. On the left side of the hallway, we had just turned into, was a bald man with stubble around his chin sitting on a silver steal chair. His hands were cuffed behind him and a police officer stood next to him. His dark almost black eyes scowled at us. As we approached them I moved closer to Jace, both our shoulders touching. He must have sensed that I was scared because he yanked on my arm. Pulling me to his right, so that I was squashed between him and Ell. I was too terrified to object .

"What's your name, beautiful?" The bald man smiled, displaying his rotting teeth. I glanced at the floor, trying to ignore him. "Your two boyfriends better keep their eyes on you cus I might just have to take you from them." He sniggered. "I like your hair... maybe when I get outta here I can come find you and run my fingers through it."

I shivered. Jace wrapped an arm around me. Glancing up at him, I saw his eyes narrow at the man. "I bet it feels like silk." He chuckled; Trying to wind up Jace, who's hands were already clenching into fists. The policeman just stood against the wall oblivious to it all.

"Oh sorry... I didn't know you wouldn't like sharing your girl." He spat sarcastically. "Your bitch might like more excitement, that's all." He winked. My stomach churned. "Don't talk about her like that." Jace snarled. The bald man smiled again, making the color in my skin drain. "You might want to put thoughs fists away, Mexican...there's a cop in the hall." He sniggered sourly.

Suddenly he fidgeted in his chair, as we passed. I jumped, stumbling into Ell who almost fell over. "It's okay Brittany." He whispered, holding me up. Thump! We turned our heads to Jace. He was on the floor. I saw the bald man's foot moving back. He must have tripped him. Jace dived at him. Tipping the chair over. Ell pulled me behind him so that I was out of their way. Jace slammed his fist into the man. The policeman seemed to awake from his daydream. The criminal shoved Jace. Thud! He fell backwards onto the floor. In a flash the man was up and kicking him.

Before Ell could get in there and help Jace out, the cop leaped in. Trying to take control of the situation; Grabbing the bald man. Jace sprung up and charged at him. The cop stepped between them, his arms spread out. Stopping the two from fighting, with his hands. He kicked the chair up and pushed the bald man towards it. Shoving him down. Then he scrunched up Jace's shirt with his fist. "Now you listen here...and you listen real good...if I catch you in this station again I'll arrest all three of you young 'in." He threatened, spitting a little. He released Jace. "You got it!" "Yeah." Jace glared, his jaw stern. "Good, now get." He ordered pointing at the glass doors at the bottom of the hall. Jace marched ahead wiping the saliva off his face as he ignored the smirking man. I tightly squeezed at Ell's hand.

The man scowled at Jace. Still and silent. No other expression except hate. His chiseled features stayed solid. Like stone. His eyes flashed to Ell. He continued to stare as we passed. His expression changed. From hate to something else. Friendlier. Happier, almost. It nearly looked like he recognized him. "I always wondered what you would look like grown up..." He smiled. Ell glanced at me, as if checking to see if I had said it. After a second he met the bald man's gaze. He was unsure. Obviously he didn't know *him*.

"Elliot...ain't it?" The man asked.

Ell's eyes widened. He was nervous about this stranger knowing his name. I noticed that Jace didn't stop. He kept walking to the door. "You don't know me now but you will." The man smiled. "you will." Ell pulled on my arm. He shivered, slightly and walked faster then his normal pace. When we stepped out into the dusk Ell let go of my hand.

CHAPTER 9

ONE MONTH LATER

JASON MARTINO

    I dipped my paintbrush into the blue acrylic paint and dragged it across the top of the page. Suddenly, the door banged against the wall. My eyes flashed to that direction. I froze. My dad stumbled in. His hands cracked as they tightened into fists. "Where'd you get those, boy?" He asked.

    I glanced at the box of paints then back to him. Silence. "I said where'd you get 'em?" He rose his voice, slightly.

    "B...Britt gave them to me." I stuttered, kicking the box under the bed secretively.

    "Liar, you must have stolen them." He yelled, lunging towards me. Before I could move he grabbed my arm. Throwing me to the floor. I crashed onto my paintbrushes. Crack!

    He went for the paint box. I tried to stop him but he pushed back with his hand. I felt like I was a wimpy four year old, not seventeen. "You're a thief!" He yelled, smashing my paint under his foot. The tube's lid shot off and red acrylic sprayed out. "I didn't raise you to be a liar and a thief!" He hollered louder.

"Dad stop!" I tried to sound strong and intimidating. My voice was louder but it was a weak and pathetic excuse for a yell. I didn't fool either of us. My dad threw the remaining paint and it's container at the wall. Smash.

"Don't you back talk me." He hissed, moving closer. He was about three steps away from me. I could smell the stench of beer. "You ungrateful piece of shit." He spat.

He rammed his fist into my stomach. "Oof." I gasped, winded. My immediate reaction was to grab my abdomen, to some how numb the pain. I didn't want him to know who much it hurt. Clenching my jaw, I ripped my hands away. He shoved hard on my shoulder. I stumbled backwards. Tripping over my own feet, I landed on the floor. "What have I told you about steeling." He leaned over me. His angry face five inches away from mine.

"What have I told you?" He bellowed.

"Martino's don't steel." My voice was hard for even me to hear. He straightened his back. "Good." He praised, almost smiling.

"Now where'd you really get them?" His voice was a little softer. I flinched at his non-blinking stare. "I...I...told you Britt.."

"Liar!" He scolded, kicking my side. His trainer smacked into my ribs over and over. Cracking them easily as if they were only twigs. Ding dong. The door bell rang. The phrase saved by the bell had never meant so much to me.

He slammed the door behind him. I raised myself up on my elbows. Wincing with every breath. 'Be strong, Jace.' I told myself. Biting through the pain, I slowly stood up. Left foot, right foot. I concentrated on walking and pushed the agony to the back of my head. My hand rubbed my throbbing side. Carefully, I sat myself on the bed.

CHAPTER 10

BRITTANY CHAPMAN

Kelly was so excited because Shannon was staying over tonight. I was excited too. Shannon meant that Ell was coming over. I hadn't seen him since November. It felt like he was avoiding me. I ran down stairs and answered the door. "Happy New Year!" Shannon grinned. "I made this for you!" She handed me a white paper card with a red crayon stickman on the front. 'Merry Christmas...sorry it's late.' it said in black. "Aww thank you Shannon it's beautiful." I smiled. She hugged me. Resting her head on my growing tummy. I ran my fingers through her beautiful light blonde hair.

She pulled away and looked back up at me. "Is Kelly in her room?"

"Yes!" I smiled. As fast as she could she hopped up the stairs. Elliot shut the door behind him. Immediately he hugged me, too. It appeared he was happier then the last time I saw him. "Hey Britt!" He smiled, struggling to keep his pitch high and friendly. "Are you ok, Ell?" I asked. His smile slipped from his face. He stared at the floor. "Most people reply with, hey Ell!" He smirked, weakly. His hands slid into his jean pockets.

ELLIOT GARDENER

I thought I could do it. I thought I could act like everything was normal and just be my old self. Seeing her brought it all back. Just then I remembered the main reason I was here. I could hear Shannon and Kelly laughing upstairs.

Glancing back up at her I said. "Oh...you should know Shannon's been having these bad nightmares that have been really freakin' her out."

"Ok." She nodded pushing her hair behind her left ear. "What should I do if she get's one?"

"She'll probably come in and tell you." "You don't mind her sleeping with you, do you?"

"No, no of course not." "Well...she doesn't talk like you, does she?" She asked, smiling.

"How did you know that?" I laughed. And just like that she had made me laugh.

"Do you remember that time we had a sleep over when we were all eleven?"

I nodded, smiling.

"Yeah, I couldn't sleep because of you." She smirked.

BRITTANY CHAPMAN

He blushed a little. "No...she doesn't talk in her sleep." We stood there for a minute smiling; Remembering the good old days. Suddenly November at the station clicked in my head. Who was that man and how did he know Ell? "Hey, umm Elliot you know that man at the police station, how did he know you? Did you figure out if you knew where he was from yet?"

"Are you still thinking' about that?" He shook his head, smiling.

"Elliot this is serious."

He snorted. "Britt, what are you talking about?"

"Don't you think that's weird how some guy knows your name and you've never seen him before, right when all this is happening?"

He didn't answer for two seconds. "No I don't know who he was…I even looked through a bunch of my mom's old photos and nothing."

Ell lifted his arm and smelled his green and white checkered sleeve. "Hey…do you think I could use your shower?" He asked, scrunching his face. I smiled. "Yeah sure." I didn't think to ask why. It wasn't too hard to guess though. His mom was working as a waitress and had two kids, their water had probably been cut. "Thanks." He breathed relieved and ran up the stairs.

I looked through my window to Jace's room. It was empty. Just a bed, and a lake of clothes, papers, books and paintbrushes that covered the floor. I sat on my bed feeling lonely, even though the house was full. My soccer ball clock said that it was 7:00pm but it looked a lot later outside.

Suddenly two screams exploded from the bathroom, next door to my room. One sounded like Tasha the other was lower pitched. Male. My door flew open. Tasha in her white knee-length skirt and red long sleeve top. "Brittany can you please explain why Elliot's in our shower?" She yelled, her face pink. I bit my lip, trying not to laugh. "He needed a shower."

"Why can't he take one at his house?"

"Why…didn't you like the view?" I laughed. Her cheeks grew pinker. "Shut up, Brittany." She hissed, slamming the door.

Later after Ell gave me an embarrassed smile and left and everyone was asleep, I laid in my bed staring at the ceiling. My covers were tightly wrapped around me but I was still cold. Something told me that it wasn't the temperature of the room. Shivering I stood and dragged my quilt to my window with me. Jace was still gone. I was starting to get worried. I tried to think about sleep. Nothing worked. Staring at the tree between our windows I watched the crow continue to work on his nest. I cuddled my quilt around me and stumbled back to my bed.

Just like Ell predicted Shannon wandered into my room. Her angelic face stained with tears. "What's wrong?" I asked, sitting up. She clambered in next to me, her arms stretched out. "I had a nightmare." She whimpered. Her head rested on my shoulder as more tears created damp patches on my pajama shirt. "Can I sleep with you?" She asked, muffled. "Sure." I scooted over to leave her space and laid on my back. Shannon wrapped her arms around my waist and rested her head on my chest. "What was it about?" I asked, patting her head.

"I've had them every night for a week...always the same one." She sniffed. "I'm playing at the park and this black van pulls up, a man asks me to come with him. He seems nice so I always go but he threw me into the back of the van. I see a gun and then it goes blurry and I wake up."

"It's ok Shan." I whispered. I decided it was better to let her sleep rather then talk more about her nightmares. At least I had someone to spend the night with. Some nights were better then others. Some nights I didn't think of November; But others (like tonight) I did, and even though I tried not to show it -for Shannon-I was scared. Her nightmare was just a dream and it couldn't really happen (could it) but it managed to give me goose bumps.

CHAPTER 11

Before I knew it school had started again. A long week of school with those ratty girls who think they're all that, the "populars", almost drove me crazy. There's a group in every school.

The ring leader to this one was, Michelle Weathersfield. She was really pretty, glossy wavy golden hair and a heart shaped face. She always had beautiful clothes and an echo to match the amount of money her parents had. Don't let her bright blue eyes fool you, she was evil. Her followers included Denise Smith, an African American who was also pretty. She normally had long straight black hair and was the same height as Michelle. Another one was a pale skinned girl who had dark brown hair with light brown highlights. It was always curly, almost a bob with little ringlets. She was a little shorter then the other two. Her name was Charlie Goldenberg.

I wandered through my house. A million baby's crying. I juggled bottles and dippers. In the living room were so many cribs that I couldn't get in. I ran up to my room, scared and confused. There in a cradle laid a tiny baby. Turning red from it's squawks and shrieks. Panting, I sat up in my bed and the clouded dream faded. I wiped the sweat from my forehead with the back of my hand. Swallowing hard I glanced at my clock. 7:45. "Oh crap!" "I'm late!" I screamed to myself. I ran around my room, throwing on clothes, make up and trying to brush my hair at the same time.

I crossed off the Friday on my calendar, 15th February. I lifted my shirt and stared at myself in the bathroom mirror. A very clear bump of four months was showing. Jason wasn't in his room, he was probably already dressed and downstairs eating breakfast. His dad wasn't home. It caught my attention that the crow's nest had gotten bigger.

The day before I bought some new clothes. My mom reluctantly drove me. Tasha came with me, bringing me clothes and pushing them up against me to see if they'd fit. She was having way to much fun. Eventually I ended up buying five new bras ranging in different sizes and some baggier shirts and jeans.

That night, during dinner, my mom decided it was time to bring up the fact that I was starting to show. "What are you going to do?" She asked, staring at my small bump. "I don't know." I replied, sipping my soup. Uselessly, hoping that was the end of it. The dinner table stayed silent for a while. Kelly, Tasha and Joe pretended the question didn't come up as I glanced at their faces. Kelly did look up to meet my glimpse. "Where do babies come from?" She asked, flicking her eyes to the head of the table.

My mom said, "We'll talk about that later, dear."

"Brittany, there is still time for you to get an abortion you know." I glared at the red tomato soup.

"You can't possibly make a decision like that by yourself!" Why was Joe getting involved. I ignored him.

"You can't actually be thinking of going through with this." "With having this...this monster." My eyes flashed to my bump.

I rubbed it gently as if the baby had been hurt. "It's not a monster." I mumbled.

"What?" "Yes it is!" She scowled.

"No it's not!" I protested, screeching the chair as I stood. We glared at each other for a moment until I decided to speak again. "None of this is it's fault!" Then I left, without really deciding where I was going. I could hear Joe muffling about something to Hilary as I walked through the hallway to the stairs.

I stared at my dad's picture, hanging on the wall. Slipping it out of it's frame a tattered piece of paper floated to the floor. I cocked my head to the side. I'd never taken it out of the frame before. I wondered how old the paper was. I picked it up and read it.

'Dear Charlie,
I've been looking for you for a while, now. It's so nice when I come across old friends. Why don't we meet up somewhere? How does our old hide out sound? You know the one where everything is dead in the middle.
I can't wait to hear how your life has changed and what new things are in it. I happened to have just moved near by with a new family of mine, hopefully our children will be friends.
I can't wait to see you again. DON'T bring company! I was hoping we could bond, ALONE!
Come find me, Mark'

I dropped the note and stumbled backwards. My arms were shaking as I wrapped them around me. At that moment my cell phone buzzed on my bed. Pushing my hair behind my ear I tried to make myself calm down.

"Hello?"
No one answered.
"Hello?" I said again, my voice dry.
Still no one answered.
"Who's there?" "Elliot is this you?"
Nothing.
"Ell if this is one of your jokes it's not funny." "H...hello"
Click. The phone went down.

CHAPTER 12

'Only two more classes.' I thought to myself, heading to Biology. Jace was already there. I sat on the stool next to him. "Your late." He whispered, passing me a text book.

"Some people have to use the restroom." I said, watching Mr. Brown to see if I could make sense of what he was saying. I heard Jace chuckle beside me.

"Aww, Miss Chapman thank you for joining us." He said. He was scribbling on the white board.

"I swear he has eyes in the back of his head." I whispered to Jace. He smiled, flipping through the pages in his book.

Someone knocked on the door. Mr. Brown pushed up his glasses as he looked to the door. The class was happy to have an excuse to stop listening to his draining speech. Elliot walked in smiling. "May I help you Mr. Gardener?"

"Yeah, well actually I'm just here to talk to Jason."

"If it's important enough to interrupt my class then I'm sure you can tell him from there."

"Okay." Ell shrugged. Jace smiled, this time with teeth.

"I was making sure that you were coming over to my house after school today."

The class wolf whistled and cheered. I heard Jace laugh beside me. His gravelly chuckle. Ell was smiling, soaking up the attention.

"Um...yeah I am." Jace grinned. They agreed that today they'd paint Shan's room. Jace loved to paint and was a pretty good artist so I bet he was going to do most of the work.

"Ok I'll meet you at my house then... can't wait." He smirked, winking.

Jace just laughed as Ell blew him a kiss.

"See you then ." Jace managed to say through his laughter.

I swear they did this to embarrass me.

I stared at the blue and white tiles of the hallway as I pulled my backpack further over my shoulder. Crowds of people walked passed me but Elliot and Jason were no where in sight. I walked passed our lockers, scanning them to see if they were there. Just my stickers and photos. I glanced up, trying to see over the heads, to find the exit door. The end of school was always this hectic. Suddenly the crowd split in two.

Almost like when Moses parted the red sea for the Jews. The "populars" were walking down the hall. Everyone had moved out of their way and made as much room as they could, squashed up against the white walls. I stood in the middle continuing to walk, to the exit at the end of the hall. They marched towards me in a horizontal line, like movie stars strutting down a red carpet. I wasn't going to step aside for them and bow down like a servant handing fruit to their master.

Michelle flicked her hair and stepped forward. "Move, Chapman!" She spat in disgust.

"Why don't you move, Weathersfield!" I frowned, my eyes narrowing.

"You did not just tell Michelle to move." Denise snapped in my face. "For your information she's the most popular girl in school." She reminded, trying break me somehow.

"Does it look like I care?" I scowled. Charlie just scowled at me in silence.

"Well, you certainly are getting fat." Michelle laughed. Strutting around me as if inspecting me. "Ha...and are those boy's jeans?" She mocked, pointing with her skinny finger.

Red nail polish that daddy probably bought for her. I pushed through the cackling sidekicks, knocking Charlie's shoulder, which was about half way down my forearm. Continuing to the exit I didn't look back, feeling all three eyes piercing into my skin. A tear drizzled down my face.

   Finally back at home, I threw my bag onto the bed. 'Thank goodness, it's the weekend tomorrow.' I thought to myself. I pressed play on my stereo and sang along with the song that came on. That always cheered me up.

   Suddenly my cell phone rang. I turned down the volume and answered. I thought it might be Elliot. "Hello?" No one answered. Goosebumps appeared on my arm. "Hello?" I said again. Still nothing. "Who…who's there?" The phone began to shake in my hand. The other end breathed heavily. "You, you…better stop calling m..me." My voice was weak. The phone clicked. I hung up too. Throwing it onto a pillow by the window. I shook, sitting on the bed. A tear rolled down my cheek.

CHAPTER 13

HILARY CHAPMAN

Mrs. Linley, a respected neighbor, came round. We sat in the living room staring at the coffee in our hands. This only meant one thing when she visited. Bad news. News that she just had to stick her nose into. Being a respected lady in our neighborhood her rumors were golden no matter how much crap they had been sprinkled with. She had probably come around because she'd heard my family was having problems and wanted to interfere.

"You know, Hilary, we hardly talk anymore..." *I wander why?* "How have you been?" That really meant what can I tell my friends about your family?

"I've been good, I suppose."

She put down her coffee on a costar, which she took the privilege to wipe down earlier. "I know about your daughter, Hilary." She said, pushing her glasses further up her pointy nose.

"Oh yeah?"

"She's getting bigger...around the waistline, you know what I mean?"

"Yes...I know."

"So it's true? Well, I hate to say I told you so." That was a lie, she loved it. Proving herself right in matters that didn't even concern her.

"I really do, but that boy has been crawling into your daughter's bedroom window for ten years now." "I knew that one day this would happen."

I didn't know what to say to that, so I said nothing. She picked up her coffee and took another sip.

"I did tell you to keep her away from that boy, 'he's trouble' I told you..." I zoned out from her muttering. Staring out the window behind her, I watched a car pull up. The pizza delivery man. He got out with the pizza and walked up to the Cutters house. He delivered pizza to us a couple times before; I think his name was Gary. "I know how hard this must be for you, dear. Your daughter pregnant with some Mexican's child." This had gone far enough. Once she was out of here, she would spread her lies to everyone else.

I stood. "That boy's name is Jason Martino and he is not the father of my daughters baby.

"Oh?"

"Frankly Mrs. Linley this has nothing to do with you and I would like you to leave, now."

She stood too. "I beg your pardon?"

"I said leave!" I raised my voice, but didn't shout. I didn't want to yell at and elderly woman.

"Fine if that's what you want, but I was only trying..."

"I said now!" I pointed to the living room door.

I knew this would happen. People would make accusations. Why couldn't Brittany just have an abortion like I told her too. How could she feel love for this...this thing?

CHAPTER 14

BRITTANY CHAPMAN

    I stared out my window waiting for Ell. Jace was looking through some of my old CDs on the floor. I gazed at the old crow. He was half way through building his nest. Snow started to fall again. "Jace it's snowing again!" I screamed excitedly as I jumped. Jace got up to join me. Once the novelty of fresh snow falling to the ground wore off, I walked across the room to check my calendar. February 16th.

    Honk, honk! We ran outside and got into Elliot's mom's rusty blue truck. "It's so cool now that you can drive!" I smiled, putting on my seatbelt. Jace slid in next to me. "I wish I could drive." He frowned. "Yeah, like they'd let you drive!" I teased. Ell laughed with me, but Jace just scowled. "Yeah but I haven't had a driving test yet."

    "But when I do I wont fail my first time unlike *some* people." He mumbled, trying to offend me by reminding me of my bad excuse of attempting to drive. "So where's Shannon?" I asked as Ell pulled out of our street.

    "Oh, she's at a friends house." He smiled.

Driving down the highway the snow became heavier. Ell turned on the radio. *"This is the coldest winter that Wilder back, Arizona has ever seen!" "Many people are saying that a blizzard is on it's way!"*

"Looks like the movies is not an option!" Jace said, staring at the snowflakes.

"*Hello,* this is Arizona!" "There's not gonna be a blizzard!" Ell scoffed. "Yeah but there's never been this much snow before, either!" Jace smiled, ignoring Ell's sudden bad mood.

Jace lowered the window and stuck his hand out. He waited until he had a handful of snow then closed the window. Ell glanced at him then smiled as he looked back at the road. Poof! Cold, wet snow stung my cheek. "Jason!" I yelled, wiping it off. "It sticks!" He laughed with his husky chuckle. "That means it's gonna stay!" I slapped him. Then he slapped me back. A frenzy of slapping occurred. "Will you too stop fighting!" Ell pretended to yell. "Don't make me turn around!"

"He started it!" I smirked as I pointed at Jace.

Without warning the truck in front, that was carrying fruit, started spinning. Ell tried to swerve; But the back hit us and we went flying. I grabbed the seat. I suddenly felt Jace's cold hand grab mine. He clamped it to the chair, his shoulders tense. Ell's face turned white. Spinning converted into rolling. All I could see was snow and trees. I didn't think we were on the road anymore. Bang! We stopped. I looked up. White was everywhere. I glanced at Jace and Ell. They had scratches and cuts on their faces but no serious injuries. We sat there for a minute. The windscreen was cracked. It stretched across the middle.

Ell grabbed a blanket from the glove compartment. Then he pulled out a flashlight. "I'm gonna see where we are!" He said unbuckling himself. Snow poured down outside. Slam! He shut the door behind him; More snow replaced his fingerprints. Snow slapped me in the face as he opened the door back up. "We're right in front of a lodge." He informed, raising his voice above the howling wind. "I think there's a fireplace inside, I couldn't really see!" "Come on, we'll freeze in here!" Jace added.

"What did you say about the blizzard again!?" Jace taunted, putting his hand to his ear; once the lodge door closed. It was small and only had two rooms, including the bathroom. It had a musty smell, like a mixture of wet dog and soil. The undersized fire place was dull and covered in cobwebs. Every inch of the four brick walls around us was smothered in dust. The wooden floor creaked as Jace ran over to the little fridge in the kitchen area. "That's just great!" He moaned.

"There's only one can of soup!" He closed the door. "And a tiny microwave." I ran over beside him. "At least there's a tap." I said. "Yes Britt cus were gonna run out of water." Ell snarled, sarcastically. "Hey, this isn't her fault!" Jace snapped. "I told you to turn round!"

"Oh so this is all my fault!" Ell yelled back.

"Yeah...it is!" Jace growled, sizing him up. "Ok you two this isn't gonna get us out of here!" I hissed, standing between them.

I looked around. "Where are we gonna sleep?" I sighed. "You don't think we're gonna be here all night, do you!?" Jace asked. "I hope not, but incase we do we need to start that fire." I instructed. Ell walked over to the only cupboard in the lodge. "There's some pillows in here!" He cried. I pulled out an old wooden chair from the bathroom and stopped in front of the fireplace. "High-ya!" I screeched, slamming it on the floor. I looked up at them. They were staring at me. "That felt good!" I smiled. They shrugged at each other, then wandered around the room and found chairs of their own. We saved a large rocking chair, which we pulled up in front of the fire.

I looked in the cupboard for other supplies. Unsuccessful, I closed the door then gazed at Jace and Ell. They were sitting in the rocking chair with Ell's blanket and the pillows he'd found. I smiled then jumped into the middle. I scrunched myself between them and snuggled into the warm blanket. Jace beamed brightly, tucking me in and plumping a pillow behind my head. Ell rocked the chair gently with his foot, closing his eyes. Taking in a quick glance out the wood framed window on our right. White. Nothing more to see then that. I shut my eyes, slipping into a deep sleep.

I awoke to the sound of the orange fire crackling and bangs on the old lodge door. It opened abruptly. A man in a heavy jacket covered in snow stood in the doorway. An eruption of cold air cooled the fire until the tame lion was no longer there. The man fought against the wind and snow to close the door. He pulled off his jacket. We all stared in shock and terror. His green eyes made my skin crawl. The dry taste of vomit lingered at the back of my throat. "Hello again!" The beast smiled. "For the last time, because now you have nowhere to run and no one to save you!" He moved closer, striding himself with pride as if he were a King. Jace pulled me into his lap and held me tight. I squeezed his shaking copper hand.

Before the monster could reach the chair Ell hurled him to the ground. He punched him. "This is for my mom!" he yelled. He hit him again. "And this is for the nine year old boy you left, who had to bring up his baby sister so that his mom could find jobs!" Once more and yelled, "And that was for Brittany!" He fell in front of the man. His anger faded into pain. "Why!" He cried. "Why did you walk away!?" The villain just smiled. Kneeling he towered over Elliot. "I met Shannon!" Ell's face turned cold and pasty. "What!?" he whispered, as he stood up slowly.

"She's a nice girl, you should've told her not to talk to strangers though!" He smiled.

Ell became panicky. "What did you do to her!?" The man just smirked and tilted his head. His green eyes twinkling as he stood gradually, like a ghost.

"Where is she!" Ell yelled, frustrated. At that moment the creature pulled out a familiar object, pointing the dagger at Ell. He glanced at the knife but remained angry.

It didn't seem to phase him. "Where is she!?" He hissed again. "Here she is!" The man pulled out a black phone. He passed it to Ell. Jace and I stood, wondering what to do.

"Shannon!" Ell exclaimed. He listened intently. "I know baby, just calm down!" "Where are you!" He paused. "What color van!?"

"Black windows!" He whispered to himself. He paused again. "Do they have guns!?" He asked. "Shan...please don't cry...I need you to be brave!" "Shannon listen to me...I'll come get you!" He wiped a tear from his cheek. "I love you, too!" Then he hung up. The beast snatched the phone back. "Why do they have guns!?" He winced, his voice braking in two places. Swallowing hard he tried to control his emotions. "Don't let them hurt her!" He demanded. The man's red eye's blazed. His crooked smile made my stomach flip.

"I'll make sure they don't lay a finger on her, if you do something for me!" He said.

"Anything, just don't hurt Shannon!" He begged.

"I want you to kill Brittany!" He glared. Ell glanced at me then back. "What!?" He mouthed.

"With this knife, in her heart!" The man placed the knife in his hand.

"Stab him!" Jace snarled.

"If you do that, then all I have to do is press this button and they'll shoot Shannon!" The bear roared. Ell swallowed then closed his eyes. In a few seconds he opened them.

He pushed the knife into his back pocket. He gazed into my eyes as he walked towards me. I was hypnotized by the liquid green poison in his stare. My feet were glued to the ground. I looked around for help. Jace froze, trying to work out what was happening. Ell wrapped his left arm around my waist then used the other to run his fingers through my hair. He closed his eyes again then slowly breathed out. He guided me down and laid me flat onto the damp wooden floor. His hand quivered as he pulled out the dagger. "Ell what are you doin!?" Jace yelled. Ell glanced at him then back. He bit his lip, then leaned over me.

"Elliot!" I whispered; My eyes pleaded with his. He looked down then back up. A tear rolled down his cheek. "She's my little sister, Britt!" He slowly and carefully undid my grey knitted sweater. At the last button the monster chuckled "I want to see the blood run from her skin when you kill her!" Ell flinched. He forced his eyes closed. His body trembled over me. He raised his left hand and pulled up my shirt. A blast of coldness tingled my stomach and stretch marks. Flash backs filled my head and washed over me. I found myself crying. The beast laughed. Jace clenched his fists. The man raised the phone as a threat. Ell glanced at the phone then at Jace, horrified. He swallowed then put his lips to my ear. "I'm sorry!" He whispered, choking on his fear.

He stared at my chest as he elevated his arm. But his focus slipped and his eyes met mine. "Kill her!" The beast roared, impatiently. Ell glanced at him. "I can't!"

The man raised the phone again.

"Please don't!" He begged. "I'll do anything else!" "Please, don't make me do this!"

"Anything!?" The beast smirked. "You'll do anything for your little sister...beautiful." "Course I already know that... cus see Elliot even though I left doesn't mean I was gone." "I watched your every move." "I made your mother move here because this is where the Chapman's live, course back then they were the Fairbrothers." What he was saying didn't make any sense.

Suddenly Jason threw himself onto the beast. He grabbed the phone and threw it across the room. The beast punched him. Jace grabbed his cheek. The man lifted his fist. "Stop!" Ell yelled. He hovered over the creature with the knife. I hadn't realized he'd moved. The monster laughed, "You wouldn't kill me!"

"Oh wouldn't I ?" He stabbed the tip of the dagger into the man's back.

"I'm your dad!" The man cried, raising his hands. Ell's face dropped. Hearing the words must have broken down the barrier he was trying to build. "He don't care about you, Ell!" Jace reminded.

"Don't listen to him, son!" The man cried as he scowled at Jace. "I'm your dad!" He whispered.

"Ell ignore him!" "Remember what he did!" Jace shouted.

"I only walked out on you and your mother because I knew I couldn't handle it!" "I didn't want you to have a father who couldn't take care of you!" He lied.

I stood up. "You don't care what happens to Ell!" I protested. One glace of the beast, shut me up! I bit hard on my lip to stop myself from screaming.

"Your dad was a murderer!" He hissed at me.

"And... your... better!" Jace snarled.

"Shut up you filthy Mexican!" He spat. "You belong with your mother!" "Rotting in the ground!"

Jace clenched his fists. He stepped forward, his jaw stern but Ell glanced at him. His eyes telling him to calm. Jace said something in Spanish, I guessed it was probably an insult. Then he breathed slowly. "Britt's dad fought for his country!" "He died in action!"
"No he didn't!" The beast smiled.
"You killed my dad!?" I screamed.
"What about Brittany?" Ell asked. "Why her?"
"Her murdering, betraying dad killed Nick! He was never in the army, he only pretended because he didn't want to admit he was working with me." My dad was working with... He was the other man distributing drugs? I couldn't believe it. How could I? No! I refused to believe that, after all look who it was coming from. It had to be a lie. I remembered the interrogation and how Investigator Gilman told Ell that there were two other men. My dad knew about the murder, how else could he have known. He was working with them; But who was the fourth man?

"You would have done the same...your my son!"
"No!" "I'm nothing like you!" Ell protested.
"You almost killed her...you're exactly like me!"
"Take that back!" "I'll never be like you!"
"Like father, like son..." His sentence trailed into silence.
The villainous snake laughed. Without warning, blood dripped from his mouth and his eyes rolled back into his head. He fell onto his knees. Then face first. The dagger stuck out of his back. I glanced at Jace. We gazed at Ell's shirt which was splattered with blood. He stared at the body. Then he closed his eyes and fell onto his knees. He put his hands in front of him and hung his head. I moved over to sit beside him. I wrapped my arms around him and rested my head on his back. He sat up. Tears were streaming down his face. He pulled me into his chest.
I will never forget that scene. The sight of the dead body. The shock and stiffness in Jace, as he stood over us. The snow tapping at the small glass windows and the blood

trickling through the cracks in the floorboards to the ashes of the fire.